D0327638

www.amazon.com/
your-account

For detailed information about this and
other orders, please visit Your Account.
You can also print invoices, change your
e-mail address and payment settings,
alter your communication preferences,
and much more - 24 hours a day - at
http://www.amazon.com/your-account.

Item Price	Total
$8.22	$16.44
$8.22	$16.44
$8.22	$16.44
$8.55	$17.10
$8.22	$16.44
	$82.86
	$4.94
	$87.80
	$87.80
	$0.00

Returns Are Easy!

Most items can be refunded, exchanged,
or replaced when returned in original
and unopened condition. Visit http://
www.amazon.com/returns to start your
return, or http://www.amazon.com/help
for more information on return policies.

Gift Cards
Millions of items. No expiration.
www.amazon.com/giftcards

Get Amazon Mobile
Fast, easy and free access
to shopping, order tracking
and more.

www.amazon.com/app

)4:29 Pack Type : A0

THE ADVENTURES OF
DANNY CRICKET

Danny Cricket Visits St. Augustine

WRITTEN BY ANNETTE R. BURRELL
ILLUSTRATED BY MARK C. COLLINS

This book is dedicated to my beach buddies Peggie, Beth, Susan and Wanda. Through the years you guys have taught me some valuable life lessons: 1) how to lie out on the beach and not get sunburned; 2) books and flip flops are all you really need at the beach; 3) you don't have to own stock in Wal-Mart to shop there every day; 4) you can meet the nicest people while changing a tire; and 5) the next best thing to Godliness is smelling the salt air and listening to the ocean waves in the morning, and watching the sun set behind those same waves in the evening.
Everyone should have girlfriends like you all.
I love you guys!!!

ISBN 10: 1489551301
ISBN 13: 978-1489551306

I'm so excited to be standing on the beach,
The waves crashing in, the sun just out of reach.

The sand is so white it's almost blinding me.
But the beauty of it all is wonderful to see.

Seagulls and seashells
Seem to be everywhere,
And there are umbrellas
Over all the beach chairs.

So since sunbathing
Isn't quite my style,
I'll just lie in the shade
And stay for a while.

I see something move
As I look at the sand,
And the suspense is just about
All that I can stand.

There are hundreds of shells,
But this one has eyes.
And it's walking toward me,
Oh what a surprise!

Big bubbly-type eyes
And legs that have claws,
He retreats to his shell
And seems to just pause.

So I try not to scare him,
I don't make a sound.
I get out of my chair -
Get close to the ground.

He peeks out again
And walks over to me.
I say, "Hey little man,
My name is Danny."

"My name is Herman,"
He quietly replies.
"I was just on my way
To go get baptized."

So I tag along
To support my new friend.
We round a corner
And de Leon joins in,

"This town's old,
Since 1565,
And the Fountain of Youth
Helps keep us alive."

"That's where I was baptized
Many years ago,
When you believe in Him,
It's the next step, you know.

So, Danny, come along
With me and Herman,
And today you'll hear
The best ever sermon."

Juan de Batiste is there
As we walk in the gate.
Says, "Come up to the fountain,
Don't hesitate."

So Herman and I
Walk up and step in.
Juan de Batiste says,
"Let the baptisms begin."

He dunks Herman first
And then turns to me.
"Baptism's for you, Danny,
And all who believe."

Then he dunks me, too,
Like he did to Herman.
He then raises his hand
And finishes his sermon.

When I open my eyes
There floating in the air,
Is Senorita Anita
Reciting the Lord's Prayer.

She heads for the lighthouse
When her job is done,
And I am right behind her
To join in the fun.

The lighthouse is enormous -
Red, black and white.
I just stop in my tracks
And take in the sight.

I'm told in the fog
The light will show you the way,
But you must be willing
To trust and obey.

I enjoyed my time here
In St Augustine,
I'd say it's the best beach town
I've ever seen.

But being baptized
Was my favorite part.
Now every creature knows
Who lives in my heart.

To be continued...

Made in the USA
Lexington, KY
07 January 2014